Is this Book Fire Proof?

Well do you know
how to start a fire?

More importantly do you know how to put out a fire?

If it's really windy
out this book might
be fire proof

I mean it's definitely fire proof under water..

Everything changed when the fire nation attacked

Disclaimer
fire is hot

Halfway through, you're on fire. Not literally.. Hopefully

Imagine being stuck
on a desert island
with this book, it
might just save you

Rip out this page
and burn it

You're a trail blazer

Light this book and then throw it… So fire flys

Hard book to get back if you lent it to someone

You're smoking hot

Congratulations this
is the end of the
book.
Flame on